WITHDRAWN

Linda Chapman lives in Leicestershire with her family and two dogs. When she is not writing, she spends her time looking after her three children, reading, talking to people about writing, and horse riding whenever she can.

You can find out more about Linda on her websites at *lindachapman.co.uk* and *lindachapmanauthor.co.uk*

Books by Linda Chapman

BRIGHT LIGHTS
CENTRE STAGE
MY SECRET UNICORN series
NOT QUITE A MERMAID series
SKATING SCHOOL series
SKY HORSES series
STARDUST series
UNICORN SCHOOL series

Skating
Scarlet Skate Magic
School

Linda Chapman

Illustrated by Nellie Ryan

PUFFIN

Madam Letsworth's Magic Ice-Skating Academy

FROST FAIRIES

MOLLY   HANNAH   EMILY   TILDA   ALICE

ICE OWLS

AMANDA   ZOE   HEATHER   TASHA   OLIVIA

SNOW FOXES

CAMILLA   TESS   CLARE   HELENA

*To Jessica Duxbury and Iola Chapman whose
enthusiasm from the beginning helped me so much*

PUFFIN BOOKS

Published by the Penguin Group
Penguin Books Ltd, 80 Strand, London WC2R 0RL, England
Penguin Group (USA) Inc., 375 Hudson Street, New York, New York 10014, USA
Penguin Group (Canada), 90 Eglinton Avenue East, Suite 700, Toronto, Ontario, Canada M4P 2Y3
(a division of Pearson Penguin Canada Inc.)
Penguin Ireland, 25 St Stephen's Green, Dublin 2, Ireland (a division of Penguin Books Ltd)
Penguin Group (Australia), 250 Camberwell Road, Camberwell, Victoria 3124, Australia
(a division of Pearson Australia Group Pty Ltd)
Penguin Books India Pvt Ltd, 11 Community Centre, Panchsheel Park, New Delhi – 110 017, India
Penguin Group (NZ), 67 Apollo Drive, Rosedale, North Shore 0632, New Zealand
(a division of Pearson New Zealand Ltd)
Penguin Books (South Africa) (Pty) Ltd, 24 Sturdee Avenue, Rosebank, Johannesburg 2196, South Africa

Penguin Books Ltd, Registered Offices: 80 Strand, London WC2R 0RL, England

puffinbooks.com

First published 2010
1

Text copyright © Linda Chapman, 2010
Illustrations copyright © Nellie Ryan, 2010
All rights reserved

The moral right of the author and illustrator has been asserted

Set in Bembo 15/22pt
Typeset by Palimpsest Book Production Limited, Grangemouth, Stirlingshire
Made and printed in England by Clays Ltd, St Ives plc

British Library Cataloguing in Publication Data
A CIP catalogue record for this book is available from the British Library

ISBN: 978-0-141-32635-1

www.greenpenguin.co.uk

Penguin Books is committed to a sustainable future
for our business, our readers and our planet.
The book in your hands is made from paper
certified by the Forest Stewardship Council.

Contents

In the Magic Land of Ice and Winter . . .

Everything looked just as it always did. A blanket of crisp snow covered the fields and meadows, towns and villages. Frozen lakes glittered in the rays of the pale sun and a mist hung over the tops of the jagged mountains. Silvery robins darted from tree to tree while white fluffy fox cubs tumbled after each other. But the ice sylphs who lived in the land knew something was different.

At the edge of the land one of the mountains had changed shape. Something had curled around it, great wings folded flat. Its dark-red scaly sides moved in and out, and every so often it would open its mouth and a great jet of fire would stream out.

At the Magic Ice-skating Academy three teachers were talking.

'The snow on the mountains is melting,' said Madame Li anxiously, glancing out of the window. 'We haven't got long.'

'Soon we will choose our Ice Princess,' said Madame Letsworth, the headteacher. 'We have to hope that she will be able to help us.'

'She will, if we choose wisely,' said Madame Longley, a tall ice sylph with grey hair.

'I wonder which girl it will be?' pondered Madame Li.

The three of them fell silent, each thinking about the fourteen girls downstairs.

Madame Letsworth looked thoughtful. 'This week's competition is going to be very interesting – very interesting indeed.'

Chapter One
Emily

Glide. Shoulders down. Chin up. Left skate, right skate. Here we go . . .

Emily reached back with the toe of her left leg and kicked it into the ice. Pushing upwards with her right leg, she left the ice, spinning round twice in the air. For a moment she felt weightless as the ice sparkled beneath her. She landed, her arms coming out to the sides. *Yes!*

she thought, grinning. A double toe loop.

There were thirteen other girls on the ice, all jumping, spinning and gliding as they enjoyed the free skating session. Emily spotted her two best friends – Hannah and Molly – on the other side of the rink. Hannah, her long blonde hair tied back in two plaits, was practising two jumps one after the other, her face determined. She turned a perfect double toe loop followed immediately by a double flip.

To Emily, both jumps looked great, but Hannah gave an annoyed shake of her head and tried again. Emily knew she would keep on trying until she got it absolutely right. Hannah was one of the best skaters at the Magic Ice-skating Academy and she practised really hard.

Maybe one day I'll be as good as she is, Emily thought.

When all the girls had been whisked away by magic from the human world to the Land of Ice and Winter, Emily had been one of the least experienced skaters. But she had practised lots and had won the competition at the end of the first week. The girls had had to perform a dance to show they were skating with their heart. It had been a wonderful feeling to win and Emily had been presented with a pair of snow-white skates with silver laces.

The second competition – and the violet skates that were the prizes that week – had been won by two of Emily's friends, Zoe and Heather, for skating the best as a team. It was now week three

and Emily wondered what the competition would be. Madame Letsworth, their headteacher, had hinted that it would involve skating outside. *I can't wait to find out what we'll be doing*, thought Emily, *and what colour skates the winner will get this time!*

She started to move round the rink again. Being at ice-skating school was wonderful. Emily could vividly remember standing in the school hall on that first day with all the other girls, listening to Madame Letsworth telling them that if they wanted to, they could stay at the ice-skating school for six weeks to learn about the land and take all sorts of different classes that would improve their skating. Madame Letsworth had explained that, at the end of that time, one of them would be chosen to be the Ice Princess, a girl who would help the ice sylphs in some way. She hadn't said how the Ice Princess would help, just that the chosen girl would perform a task and, if successful, would be granted her heart's desire.

Emily's blades carved neatly across the ice. As she moved smoothly and swiftly, skating in a way she had only dreamt about before she came to this magic land, she smiled happily. She might not be the best at the Academy at doing difficult spins or jumps, but no one else could possibly love skating more than she did!

Molly was spinning round on the spot nearby. Emily slowed down to watch. Her friend stopped with her hands up, her straight black hair falling like a curtain to her shoulders. Catching sight of Emily, she waved and together they skated over to Hannah.

'I just can't get this double-double combination right,' Hannah said in frustration when they reached her.

'It looks really good to me,' said Emily.

'Not good enough,' Hannah sighed.

'Forget about it. Let's play follow-my-leader instead,' said Molly. 'I'll be leader!'

'Oh, OK,' said Hannah. 'I could do with a quick break, I guess.'

Molly set off, at first quite sensibly, making them skate with one foot in the air and then with their hands on their head, but after that she made them pretend to be elephants waving their trunks.

Tilda and Alice, who shared a dorm with them, joined in and Molly made

them all be chickens, pretending to lay
eggs. Soon they were giggling so much
they could hardly stand up.

A pretty girl with strawberry-blonde
hair glided past. 'You lot are *so* immature,'
she said witheringly.

Molly opened her eyes wide. 'Camilla,
did you eat a lemon at lunchtime?'

Camilla frowned. 'Of course not. Why?'

'I just thought you must have done
because your face is so sour!' Molly said
with a grin.

Camilla glared at her and skated off.

Emily wished she was more like Molly. She never seemed to mind what people thought of her, but Emily hated it if people didn't like her or were mean to her.

Just then, Madame Letsworth appeared beside the rink and blew a whistle. 'Time to get changed, girls. I've got an announcement to make.'

'Do you think we're about to find out what the competition will be?' Hannah said, looking at the others.

'And what colour the skates will be this week?' added Tilda.

Excitement rushed through Emily. 'I hope so.'

'Come on!' cried Molly. 'Last one off the ice is a squashed tomato!'

Chapter Two
The Competition

The girls got changed. Most days they wore simple skating dresses, tights and wrap-over cardigans, but for the competitions at the end of each week they often had special outfits that the frost fairies made. The frost fairies were tiny creatures who helped look after everything in the Magic Ice-skating Academy. Emily loved them. Their voices were too high for her to understand, but she would often go down to the rink and sit quietly, letting them perch on her shoulders and arms, their delicate wings fluttering.

When everyone was ready, Madame Letsworth held up her hand for silence. 'It's time to tell you about this week's competition, girls,' she announced.

There was a buzz of excited chatter. Madame Letsworth waited for it to die down. 'This week,' she said, when everyone was giving her their full attention, 'the winners will each receive a pair of scarlet skates with silver laces.' She pulled a pair of skates out of a bag beside her. They were a glowing red with glittering silver laces and fastenings.

Emily gazed at them. They were beautiful.

'This competition will be a test of your resourcefulness and courage. We want to see how well you cope in the land outside,' Madame Letsworth went on. 'And so you will be going on a two-day scavenger hunt. This will involve skating and cross-country skiing, using a map to

get through the woods and the foothills of the mountains as you try and find five special things. You will work together in teams of three or four.'

Emily caught her breath. What an amazing competition!

Amanda, a pretty girl with long dark hair, didn't seem to think so. She was staring at Madame Letsworth in horror. 'We're going to be outside for two whole days! But it'll be cold and —'

'Will we be able to choose our own teams?' interrupted Camilla.

'Yes, you will,' Madame Letsworth replied.

'We're a team!' Molly whispered immediately. Emily and Hannah nodded. All around them, people started to talk to their best friends.

Amanda kept on. 'Do we *have* to go? Can't we stay here?'

'You'll enjoy it, Amanda,' Madame Letsworth told her briskly. 'And yes, everyone has to go. Quiet now, please, girls. You can sort out your teams in a minute. First, a few more details. The scavenger hunt will take place on Thursday and Friday. You will carry rucksacks with changes of clothes, maps and food.'

'Will we be camping out in tents?' asked Zoe, who was in the Ice Owls dorm.

'No, each team will have their own shelter in the woods with sleeping bags, food, a stove and a heater.'

Hannah put her hand up. 'What things will we have to find, Madame?'

'A feather from an ice owl, an

unmeltable icicle from the Starlight
Caves, a reed from the Rainbow Pools
and a leaf from a burning bush,' replied
Madame Letsworth. 'And finally you
must also find out one new fact about the
land that you have not been told about in
a lesson.' She smiled round at them all.
'Now you may decide on your teams.'

Tilda and Alice immediately pounced

on Emily. 'Will you come in a team with us, Em?' Tilda asked.

'I can't,' Emily said quickly. 'I'm with Molly and Hannah. Why don't you ask Heather or Zoe? They're really nice.'

'Good idea,' said Tilda. 'We'll ask both of them!'

Two of the other Ice Owls had made a pair – Olivia and Tasha. Emily saw them hesitate and then reluctantly include Amanda, who was in their dorm too. Camilla had made a team with her three friends: Helena, Clare and Tess. They were all in the Snow Foxes dorm.

'We've got the best team,' Molly declared gleefully to Emily and Hannah. 'We are *so* going to win.'

'In your dreams, Molly!' Camilla snorted. She held up her hand and the others in her team high-fived with her. 'Snow Foxes rule OK!'

Molly raised her eyebrows. 'Snow Foxes *lose* OK,' she muttered to Emily.

Emily giggled. Looking round, she realized that Hannah wasn't looking as excited as her and Molly. 'You're very quiet. What's up?' she asked.

Hannah bit her lip. 'It all sounds a bit dangerous, doesn't it? Being out on our own with no teachers and no one in charge. What if something goes wrong?'

Madame Letsworth overheard. 'This challenge is supposed to test your resourcefulness and courage, but don't worry, Hannah. You will be given a way to contact us if you're in real need.'

'It's going to be really cool,' Molly reassured her. 'Ice cool!'

Hannah took a deep breath and smiled. 'Yeah,' she replied. But she didn't look convinced.

At the Magic Ice-skating Academy, the girls had regular lessons about the Land of Ice and Winter, where they learnt all about the land they were staying in.

Emily knew that some of the girls like Camilla and Tess thought these lessons were boring, but she loved them. Madame Longley, their teacher, often brought in creatures for them to see – they had met tiny ice dragons and a snow fox. Madame Longley had also told them about some of the bigger creatures, like ice monsters, mountain lions and fire dragons – huge dragons with fiery breath who skirted the land on their way to other places.

Later that day, Madame Longley unfolded a large map in the bright, airy classroom and pinned it to the wall behind her. 'Today we will be thinking about the geography of the land. Look at this section of the map,' she said, circling a large area to the north of the school that included a forest and a mountain

LAND OF ICE AND WINTER

range. 'This is where you'll be going for your scavenger hunt.'

Emily leant forward eagerly. She didn't want to miss a single thing in case it might help in the competition.

Madame Longley started to tell them about the Starlight Caves – icicle-filled caves lit by glowing crystals in their roofs, about burning bushes that leapt with strange golden flames, and about how ice owls were moody birds and had to be approached with caution. Then she pointed out the various places on the map.

'These are the Starlight Caves and these are the Rainbow Pools,' she said, indicating two areas in the foothills of the mountains. 'As you can see, the woods between the school and the mountains are thick. There are three main rivers that run down from the mountains through the woods and into the lake at the back of the school. There are also many smaller rivers that branch off. The maps you will be given are marked to show any rivers that you can skate along and any areas where it is safe to ski across country. You will have to make sure you stick to the marked areas. There are ravines and cliffs in the woods – steep drops that you can come across suddenly if you go off the paths. You must be careful.'

'Oh, we will be,' Hannah muttered to Emily.

Chapter Three
Getting Ready to Go

For the rest of the day, all everyone talked
about was the competition. The maps
were given out after supper. Hannah
spent ages poring over her copy, chewing
her thumb as she tried to work out the
best – and safest – route to take.
Meanwhile Amanda just sat on one of the
sofas in the common room and moaned.

'I just don't see why we have to go

outside. This is supposed to be an ice-skating school, isn't it, so why do we have to go skiing and stuff?' She looked around. No one was really listening. Amanda pouted. 'I hate getting cold and I hate getting wet. It's not fair and . . .'

'Oh, Amanda, be quiet,' Camilla groaned. 'You're giving me a headache!'

For once, Emily had to agree with her.

The door opened and Madame Letsworth came in. 'How are you all getting on with your maps? Any questions?'

'Do we have to go?' Amanda said plaintively. She gave a little cough and held her hand against her chest. 'I get colds really easily. At home, my mum doesn't let me outside when it's freezing. She says it's bad for me and —'

'You'll be fine, Amanda,' Madame
Letsworth cut in.

'But . . .'

'No buts. You'll be going out with the
others and that's that.' Amanda turned
away sulkily. 'So, any questions?' Madame
Letsworth asked.

Zoe put up her hand. 'Do we have to
stay in our own shelter? Or can we visit
the other teams?'

'We don't want anyone leaving their

shelter after dark,' answered Madame Letsworth. 'It would be too dangerous – you could get lost in the woods. So the answer is no.'

She walked around checking everyone was OK and then left.

'Right,' Hannah announced to Molly and Emily, her brow furrowed. 'I think I've got a plan now. It will be most sensible to go to the furthest point first and then work our way back. That means going all the way to the Starlight Caves and then coming back by the Rainbow Pools before going to where the ice owls nest in the woods.' She pointed to where 'Ice Owls' was marked in some trees. 'And after that, we can find our shelter for the night.' There was a small hut marked with a star. 'Then the next day, we get a leaf from one of the burning bushes that grow over here.' She indicated the place on the map. 'And last of all, we come back to school.'

'Hopefully getting here first,' Molly added.

Emily nodded and glanced round the room.

Nearby, Camilla was talking quickly to her team in a low voice. She saw Emily watching. 'Are you listening?'

'No,' Emily said quickly.

'You'd better not be,' Camilla snorted. 'We're going to win this. Go Snow Foxes!'

She held up her hand in a high five and the others hit her palm with theirs.

'Is that all you four ever do?' Molly said, rolling her eyes. She mimicked Camilla's voice: 'Go Snow Foxes!' she

said, putting her hand up in a high five too. She giggled.

'Go and look in the mirror and you know what you'll see, Molly? A great big loser!' said Camilla. She turned haughtily to her friends. 'Come on, let's get out of here.' They all left the common room.

Molly shook her head. 'We have to beat them. We'll never hear the last of it if they win this competition. Have you got some sneaky short cuts planned, Hannah?'

'Oh, no,' Hannah said hastily. 'We're not taking short cuts – well, only safe ones marked on the map.'

Molly groaned. 'Hannah, we'll never win if we play it safe.'

Emily shook her head as they started to argue and sank back into the sofa. She shut her eyes and imagined all the amazing things they were going to see and do. Whether they won or not, one thing was for sure – they were going to have fun!

When Emily woke up the next morning, the others were all asleep. She decided to go to the ice rink. She loved skating when there was no one else around. Pulling on her clothes, which had been washed and neatly folded by the frost fairies, she hurried down to the rink.

The early-morning sun was shining through the domed glass roof. The ice was sparkling, perfectly smooth and white. Emily's feet itched to get on to it. As she opened her locker, she hesitated. Which boots should she wear? She had two pairs, her usual slightly battered boots that she wore for lessons and practising, and the snow-white ones she had won in the first week's competition. Emily didn't wear them most of the time because she didn't want people to think she was showing off, but when she was on her own, she loved to put them on. Now she took them out and did up the silver laces.

After warming up with some stretching exercises, Emily skated a few times round

the rink, practising gliding for as long as
she could between steps. The only sound
was the swishing of her blades as they
moved across the ice. It was so wonderful
to be there on her own. Joy filled her and
she sped up. She lifted into a single axel
jump and then threw her arms back into a
layback spin, the world blurring around
her. As she came out of it, she stumbled,
but she didn't care. She felt wonderful.
What a perfect way to start the day!

Emily skated over to the music box at
the side of the rink. At first, she had
thought the music box was run on
electricity like a CD player at home, but it
wasn't at all. She lifted the lid. Inside was a
complicated system of levers and wheels
and three small silvery-blue ice dragons.
They were asleep, curled up together in a

happy heap on the floor, but, as she looked inside, their eyes opened and they chirruped when they saw her.

Emily loved the ice dragons and had been trying to learn their language. She chirruped a *hello* back.

The dragon on the top of the heap gave her a toothy grin and flew into the air.

How are you? Emily tried to say in dragon language as he hovered by her face.

The dragon whistled back.

'We're going on a scavenger hunt tomorrow in teams.' Emily broke into English and told the dragons all about it. They started whistling and squeaking excitedly. She tried to work out what they were saying. 'I should look out for . . . ?' She couldn't quite understand.

The dragon by her head flew down to

the ice. Using the end of his pointed tail he drew a picture on the ice. Emily saw he was drawing some trees with nests in and little dragons flying about.

'You're trying to tell me there will be dragons like you in the forest?' she guessed.

All three dragons nodded eagerly.

Emily grinned. 'Cool! I was hoping

there might be. I'll come back afterwards and tell you all about it.'

Just then, she heard voices and saw Hannah and Molly coming down to the rink. They waved at her and got their skates on too. Emily changed back into her old practice skates and soon all three of them were skating around.

Hannah started practising her double toe loop–double flip combination again. It didn't look as if it was getting better; if anything, she seemed to be making more mistakes.

'She's trying too hard,' said Molly as Hannah wobbled on her landing and exclaimed in frustration.

'Hannah!' Emily went round the rink to where Hannah was skating. 'Why don't you do something else for a bit?'

'No. I want to get this right and we're going to be off the rink for two days with this competition. I wish we didn't have to go. I'd rather just be skating here.'

With a determined look on her face, Hannah skated off. Emily watched her. She had a feeling it was going to be good for Hannah to get away from the rink for a few days. Hannah took everything to do with skating so seriously, which was great, but not when she got so stressed about it. Emily watched her try the jumps again. Hannah might not be looking forward to the scavenger hunt, but *she* couldn't wait!

Chapter Four
On Their Way!

'Come on!' Molly bounced up and down on the spot on the morning of the scavenger hunt. 'Let's go and have breakfast and get our rucksacks!'

They had all been given their equipment for the trip – cross-country skis and boots, outdoor skates, packets of dried food, a torch, a penknife, a compass, a sleeping bag, matches and a small magic crystal ball. If someone was in trouble, all they had to do was rub the ball in their hands for ten seconds, breathe on it and then, as the mist cleared, they would be able to see one of the teachers back at school and talk to them. *'Day or night, your call will be answered,'* Madame Letsworth had told them. *'Use them only in*

*an emergency though. We want to see how you
cope without our assistance.'*

Everyone was down at breakfast early
that day. There was a loud buzz of
excitement in the air. Emily didn't feel
like eating at all, but Hannah made her.
'We'll get hungry and have to stop sooner
if we don't eat now,' she said sensibly.

Emily forced down a piece of toast
though it tasted like cardboard in her
mouth. She just wanted to set off!

As soon as breakfast was over, the girls
put on their warm coats and trousers,
scarves, gloves and hats and then hauled
on their rucksacks. Last of all, they
helped each other tie their cross-country
skis and boots to the rucksacks and then
they were ready.

They all made their way to the lake at

the back of the school. Three rivers ran
into it from the mountains. The girls
would all start on the North River until
they reached the woods and then they
could choose their own way, staying on
the main river or setting off down the
smaller rivers, which were marked on the
maps.

Everyone milled around on the ice,
getting used to skating with rucksacks on
their backs.

'This feels weird!' Molly said as she tried to experiment skating backwards and doing a turn. 'Whoa!' Her arms flailed and she fell over with a bump.

Emily pulled her to her feet. 'Maybe you should just try going in a straight line first,' she said, grinning.

'I can't do this!' Amanda was moaning. 'My rucksack's too heavy. The straps hurt.'

Madame Letsworth, who was standing with the other teachers – Madame Longley, Madame Li and Monsieur Carvallio, blew a whistle. 'OK, girls. It's almost time to go,' she said, checking her watch. 'Remember, first team back here tomorrow morning with all the things wins. Some of the items may be more difficult to get than others and will take a bit of working out, but that is part of the test.' She smiled. 'A little clue for one of them – sometimes it can help to listen.'

The girls all exchanged mystified glances.

'What does that mean?' Hannah muttered. But Emily had no idea.

'All right. Are you ready? Good luck, everyone! On your marks, get set, go!' Madame Letsworth declared. And they were off!

It was difficult to skate at first with so many people all together on the river. But after five minutes they reached the woods and the teams started splitting off in different directions.

'See you at the finish line, losers!' Camilla called mockingly to Emily's team. 'And when you get there, we'll already be collecting our scarlet skates.'

Her teammates giggled.

'Ignore them,' Hannah said sensibly. The Snow Foxes skated off down a small river to the left and Hannah pointed ahead. 'We'll just stay on this river,' she told Emily and Molly. 'It should take us all the way through the woods to where the mountains start.'

Emily frowned. The main river ran pretty much straight through the trees

heading north. But the Starlight Caves and Rainbow Pools in the foothills of the mountains were more to the east. 'But don't we need to go more in that direction?' She nodded through the trees.

'That's the most direct way,' Hannah agreed. 'But the rivers that go that way are small and there's no guarantee we'd be able to skate down them all. They might be blocked in some way. I think it's safer if we stay on this river. At least we'll be able to skate all the way there and not have to stop or turn round.'

'I think we should go the faster way,' argued Molly. 'If it's blocked, we'll find some other way.'

Hannah shook her head. 'My way's safer.'

Molly looked mutinous.

Emily spoke quickly. 'We can always

take smaller rivers later. Let's just get to the mountains safely and get the reed and the unmeltable icicle.'

Molly sighed. 'OK.'

The air was icy and their breath came out in little puffs. It was quiet and peaceful with the trees on either side of them. 'Look there!' Emily pointed out two white snow foxes rolling in the snow on the bank ahead.

'I love being outside like this,' Molly said happily.

Emily looked at Hannah, who grinned. 'It is rather cool,' she admitted.

It took nearly all morning for the girls to reach the edge of the woods. After a couple of hours, including a biscuit break and an early lunch of sandwiches, dried

fruit and chocolate, at long last they got
close to the foothills of the craggy
mountains. The peaks were so high they
were hidden by the clouds. Flat meadows
covered with snow spanned the area
between the trees and the mountains.

'The Starlight Caves are round the side
of the mountains over there to the east,'
Hannah said, pointing to the right. 'We
need to put our skis on now.'

They swapped their ice skates for boots,
skis and poles. Soon they were swishing
across the thick flat snow. Emily had
never been cross-country skiing until she
had started at the Ice-skating Academy.
You had to slide your skis over the snow,
using the poles to help you along.

It was a bit like skating, but much harder
work, and the girls were soon flushed and

47

out of breath. Emily wiped her glove across her face and pulled off her scarf, pushing it into her pocket. 'I'm hot.'

'Me too,' puffed Hannah. 'It's partly the skiing, but also the air's not as cold here.'

Emily realized she was right. Their breath was no longer freezing in white clouds and although she had taken her scarf off, the cold did not seem to be biting into her skin the way it usually did.

'There are some green buds on those trees over there,' Molly pointed out.

'This is really strange,' said Hannah. 'It's usually colder in mountains, isn't it?'

A memory stirred in Emily's head. She hesitated, not wanting to sound silly. 'Do you remember we had a lesson about fire dragons once with Madame Longley?' she said slowly. 'She told us about

massive dragons who breathe fire and fly round the land and sometimes stop on mountains, and how that wasn't good because their breath melted things . . .' She looked from Molly to Hannah.

'What – you think it might be warmer because of a dragon?' Molly said.

Emily shrugged. 'I don't know. But Madame Longley did say that we might get to meet a fire dragon one day.'

'I remember,' said Hannah, nodding. 'We thought she might be talking about the person who is going to be the Ice Princess.'

'Do you think it is?' said Emily. Since they had arrived at the school, they hadn't been told anything more about the Ice Princess. They didn't know what she was going to have to do or how she was going to be chosen, although they did think that it might have something to do with the competitions.

Molly's eyes lit up. 'I know! Let's go exploring in the mountains. If there is a dragon, maybe we'll see it!'

'No way,' Hannah said quickly.

'But . . .'

'No, Molly!' Hannah shook her head. 'It would be too dangerous. We haven't got any of the right stuff for going up a mountain. Anyway, I thought you wanted to win this competition? If you do, we need to get back to school as quickly as possible.'

Molly looked torn.

'Hannah's right,' Emily said. 'We'll never win if we start going into the mountains now.'

'If we go exploring and get into trouble, they might even send us home,' added Hannah.

'All right.' Molly gave a wistful look at the mountain, but gave in. 'Let's just concentrate on the competition for now.' She started to ski faster. 'Starlight Caves, here we come!'

Chapter Five
Listening

The Starlight Caves were on the lower slopes of the mountains. They looked dark and very cold inside. Emily, Hannah and Molly peered into one. 'Where are the icicles and the shining crystals Madame Longley told us about?' Molly said, frowning.

'Maybe these aren't the right caves,' Emily said.

'No, they are.' Hannah checked the
map. 'They definitely are.'

'Perhaps we just need to go further in
then,' suggested Emily.

They got their torches out and walked
cautiously into the cave.

There was a faint humming sound in
the air around them. 'What's that noise?'
Emily asked.

Molly shrugged.

'I don't like this,' said Hannah, looking
around.

'Let's try going down that way,' said Molly, pointing to a tunnel that led off the back of the cave.

It was very narrow and they could only just fit in it by ducking down. The humming grew louder as they edged along, the cold rock scraping at their clothes.

'Maybe we should go back,' Hannah started to say. 'Try –' She broke off with a gasp as the tunnel opened out into another cave. But this one was totally different!

Shining crystals studded the rocky ceiling. They glowed with their own inner light, sparkling like stars. Inside the cave were more icicles than Emily had ever seen. They hung down in strange glittering shapes. The air was alive with humming.

'Oh, wow!' Emily breathed. Her voice

was drowned out by the sound. It was as
if a whole choir of people, standing in a
vast hall, were humming different notes.
It was beautiful and magical, but almost
unbearably loud.

Molly put her hands to her ears.
'What's making that sound?'

'I think it's the icicles.' Emily took a
step towards the nearest one and listened.
It was definitely humming a note!

'Weird.' Hannah looked around. 'I'm not
sure I like it. Which icicle should we take?'

'How about this one?' Emily took hold
of one, but she couldn't break it off.

'Here, let me have a go.' Hannah
struggled with it for a few moments and
then Molly tried, but none of them
could snap it.

'Let's try a thinner one,' suggested Emily.

But no matter how hard they pulled and tugged at any of the icicles, they had no luck.

'They should be called unbreakable icicles, not unmeltable!' Molly said in dismay. 'What are we going to do?'

'Let's go outside and think about it.' Hannah shook her head. 'I can't concentrate with all this noise.'

She and Molly turned to go, but Emily stopped them. 'Wait.' She was remembering what Madame Letsworth had said as they had all left: *sometimes it can help to listen.* 'Just a minute.' Emily shut her eyes. Would she work out what to do if she just listened as Madame Letsworth had said? But all she could hear was the humming of the different icicles.

Humming . . .

She caught her breath.

'What are you doing, Em?' Molly demanded.

'Listening. Shh. I might have an idea.'

Emily put her hand on the icicle nearest to her, shut her eyes again and concentrated on the sound it was making. She wasn't sure if her plan would work, but it was worth a try and something inside her seemed to be telling her to follow her hunch. She listened hard and, after a few seconds, she started to hum herself, matching the note the icicle was making.

SNAP!

The icicle broke away from the rock and came off in her hand. Hannah and Molly gasped.

Emily stared. 'I did it!'

'But what *did* you do?' asked Hannah.

'I hummed the same note as the icicle,' replied Emily. 'It was like Madame Letsworth said. All we had to do was listen!'

'You're brilliant!' Molly said, hugging her.

'Totally! I'd never have thought of that,' Hannah said, looking at Emily in astonishment.

Emily felt a happy glow. 'It just came to me. I don't know why.'

'Well, I'm glad it did. Come on, let's get out of here,' said Hannah.

Once back in the snowy landscape, they put the icicle inside one of the pockets of Emily's rucksack. 'One item down!' said Molly, finding a pen and ticking the icicle off the list of objects at the side of the map.

'Now, we have to go to the Rainbow Pools,' said Hannah. 'They're just round the mountain to the east. We can ski there.'

It didn't take them long to reach the Rainbow Pools – seven pools between the mountains and the forest. The pools were heated by hot springs and so steam rose off them. Each was a different colour.

Hannah glanced at the banks of reeds

fringing the water. 'I hope getting a reed isn't as difficult as getting an icicle,' she said anxiously.

Molly got her penknife out of her bag. 'Only one way to find out!' She walked over and grabbed a reed. To their relief, she managed to cut it very easily.

'Look, someone else has been here already!' Emily said, spotting footprints in the snow around the reed banks. 'I wonder which team it was.'

'We'd better get a move on,' said Molly, putting the reed in Emily's rucksack with

the icicle. 'We've still got to get the feather
and find the shelter this afternoon.' She
looked at the sky. It was well past midday
and the sun was heading down in the sky.

Hannah checked the map. 'Right, the
ice owls are just south of here.' She
pointed across the field to where the
woods started. 'They're through the trees
that way, but that area is not marked as
safe on the map. I guess what we need to
do is go back the way we came and get
on the main river again.'

'But that's a really long way round,'
Emily said. 'We don't have to go all the
way back there, do we? We could use one
of the smaller rivers marked on the map.'

'Or, even better, just cut across the
fields here, go into the woods and ski
until we find a river,' said Molly.

'We can't do that,' protested Hannah. 'We're supposed to stay in the marked areas. You know that.'

'It'll be fine,' said Molly. 'It will be much quicker than going back.'

'No,' Hannah said.

'Yes!' said Molly.

'Don't argue, you two,' Emily begged, but Molly and Hannah both ignored her.

'We're staying in the areas marked on the map,' said Hannah stubbornly.

'Maybe you are, but I'm not!' Molly said equally stubbornly. 'I'm going this way!'

'No, Molly!' Emily said quickly as Molly set off.

'Molly, come back,' Hannah called in alarm. 'You can't just go off on your own.'

'You'd better come with me then,' Molly cried over her shoulder.

'Come on,' Emily urged Hannah as Molly skied off across the meadow.

'She'll come back,' Hannah replied. 'She won't really try and get there on her own.'

'Hannah! How well do you know Molly? You know what she's like when she gets like this,' Emily said. 'She's not going to come back.'

Hannah hesitated.

'Please! Come on!' Emily pleaded.

Hannah gave in. 'Oh, all right.'

'Molly, wait!' Emily called.

But Molly was too far ahead to hear them. She entered the woods without looking back.

Emily and Hannah headed after her towards the treeline. Suddenly they heard a loud scream.

They looked at each other. 'Molly!' they both gasped.

Chapter Six
Off the Path

'Molly!' Hannah shouted again, but there was no reply.

'Quick!' exclaimed Emily, her heart hammering.

They reached the trees. But just as they skied into them, Hannah grabbed Emily's arm. 'Careful, Em!' she shrieked.

In front of them, the ground ended in a steep drop. Another metre and they would

have plunged right over the edge. Emily
felt as if she'd just had a bucket of ice
dumped over her as Hannah pointed
wordlessly to a thick track in the snow.
Two ski marks came to an abrupt end and
then there was a path of flattened snow
running down the slope as if someone had
fallen and rolled over and over down it.

'Molly must have skied straight over
the edge. Come on!' Hannah was already
undoing her skis. Emily quickly did the

same. They both knew it was hard to ski downhill in cross-country skis and the slope was way too steep for them to be able to do it safely. Throwing down their rucksacks beside their skis, they began to clamber down the slope as fast as they could, grabbing on to bushes and tree trunks as they went to stop themselves from falling. All sorts of images ran through Emily's mind – Molly injured, crashed into a tree, hurt . . .

'Where is she?' Emily panted as they followed Molly's trail in the snow.

'There's one of her skis!' cried Hannah, spotting it sticking up in the snow. 'Molly! Molly!' she shouted.

Emily joined in.

A faint cry echoed from further down the slope. '*Help!*'

They scrambled towards the sound and suddenly they saw Molly.

'Oh, no!' Emily gasped.

Molly was hanging on to a tree trunk with both hands, the weight of her rucksack pulling her down the steep icy slope. Her teeth were gritted and her face was pale with the effort of clinging on.

'Hang on! We're coming!' shouted Hannah.

Within seconds, Emily and Hannah had reached Molly. Throwing themselves on the ground, they each grabbed one of her arms.

'Thank you!' Molly gasped.

Using all the strength they had, Emily and Hannah pulled Molly and her rucksack back up to safer ground.

Molly collapsed in a heap in the snow.

'Oh, Molly!' Emily said, flinging her arms round her. Hannah joined in. All three of them were shaking.

'Thank you for rescuing me!' gasped Molly, her teeth chattering with shock and cold.

For a moment they were all silent as they struggled to get their breath back. They were halfway down the steep slope. There were trees at the bottom and through them the frozen waters of a river sparkled. To the left was the drop that Molly had almost fallen over.

'Are you all right?' Emily asked Molly. 'Did you hurt yourself?'

'No. I'm OK,' said Molly.

'What happened?' Hannah demanded.

'I skated over the edge of the slope,' Molly replied. 'I was going so fast I couldn't stop in time and suddenly I was over the top of it and falling. I rolled down and down and grabbed the tree trunk just in time.' She shivered. 'Thank you so much for helping me. I didn't think I was going to be able to hold on for much longer –' She broke off. 'I should never have gone off like that,' she whispered.

'It was really dumb,' Emily agreed,
hugging her. 'Don't do it again. Not ever!'

'I won't. I promise,' said Molly. 'I just
couldn't bear the thought of skiing all the
way back round the mountain again.'

Suddenly a low hooting sound echoed
through the air. Emily glanced up and
saw a large white bird take off from a tree
nearby. 'An ice owl!' she said. 'Look!'

'He must be out hunting,' said Hannah.

The bird flew over their heads and landed on another tree where there was a large nest. It stood on the edge of the nest and shook itself. As it did so, one of its white and grey feathers spiralled to the ground.

Emily jumped to her feet and ran to where the feather had landed on the snow. She picked it up.

'Cool!' said Molly in delight.

Hannah grinned. 'You know, Molly, maybe coming off the map was a good thing to do after all!'

'Ha! Didn't you know, it was my plan all along!' Molly said airily. She grinned back at Hannah. 'But, you know, I think we should maybe stick to the map from now on!'

Chapter Seven
The Ice Ghost

Hannah got to her feet, offering Molly a
hand up. 'Emily and I will have to go
and get our rucksacks and things.' She
checked the map. 'But then, if we walk
down through the trees here, we should
soon get to a river that is marked on the
map.'

'Will it take us to our shelter?' said
Emily. The thought of sitting down

inside, lighting a fire and having a rest seemed very appealing.

Hannah nodded.

'We can tell ghost stories when we're there,' said Molly as they started to tramp back up the hill. 'Have you heard about the ice ghost who haunts these woods?'

'An ice ghost?' Emily said. She saw Molly's teasing glint. 'There isn't really one, is there?'

'Maybe not,' Molly admitted. 'But I bet I could make up some good stories about it! I know loads of ghost stories!'

Emily and Hannah collected their things and then all three scrambled down the slope carefully to the nearby river that was marked on the map. They put on their ice skates and skated along it for a while before switching back to their skis and setting off through the trees. They passed two other shelters on the way. One was empty and Camilla's team was in the other. Camilla was outside and she saw Emily, Hannah and Molly skiing past.

'Bet you haven't got as many things as we have!' she called as they slowed down. 'We've already got the feather, the reed and the icicle. And the icicle is really difficult to get.'

'I know. We've got one too,' said Molly.
'And we've got the other things.'

'Have you got the leaf yet?' said
Camilla, looking suddenly anxious.

'No,' said Molly. 'But we will and we'll
get back to school first tomorrow.'

Camilla snorted. 'In your dreams!'

'Come on,' Emily said to Molly. She
didn't want to waste a single second of
their adventure arguing with Camilla.

They skied on and found their hut.
It was made of logs and nestled among
the trees. Emily stopped in relief in front
of the door. Her feet were aching.
'Ouch,' she said, rubbing her toes. 'I
don't think I've ever skated so much in
one day.'

'Me neither,' said Molly. 'My legs are
aching.'

Hannah grinned at them. 'You both sound like moaning Amandas. Come on, let's go and see inside our shelter.'

It was lovely to step inside the cosy hut. There was a rug on the floor and a stove already made up with logs and coal that they just had to light. Three beds folded down from the walls. The girls got their sleeping bags out and laid them on the beds. There was a tiny kitchen with a sink and a cupboard. Beside the sink was a large dish full of sausages and beans, three big red apples and a chocolate cake.

They each had a piece of cake and then unpacked. The stove soon warmed the shelter up.

'This is brilliant,' said Molly, bouncing on her bed.

While Hannah started to heat the food on the stove, Emily went to the window of the shelter. The sun was setting and it was almost dusk. She looked out at the trees and saw something. 'There are ice dragons out there!'

The others ran up to the window. In the trees nearby were two large messy nests made with big twigs and a dragon was circling round the branches. 'I've got to go and say hello!' said Emily.

'But it's cold,' protested Molly.

'I don't care!' Emily started to pull on her coat and boots.

'Mad!' said Hannah, shaking her head.

Emily grinned and went to the door. She couldn't resist a chance to see the wild dragons.

She went outside into the snow. After the warmth of the shelter, the icy air bit into her face. She hurried over to the trees where the dragons' nests were. Two of them flew out when they saw her. She held out her hands and they flapped over and landed on her gloves, twitching their horns and chirruping.

'*Hello*,' she chirruped back in dragon language.

They both looked very startled.

'*I'm Emily,*' she told them.

They talked quickly. Emily could just about understand. '*Yes, we're the human girls from the school,*' she said and then broke into English. 'Sorry, I'm not very good at speaking dragon. I'm trying to learn it from the ice dragons at school, but it's not easy! We're here on a scavenger hunt. There are four teams of us.' The dragons nodded. They seemed to understand her just like the dragons at the school did. 'We've got to get four things.' Emily told them all about the objects they had to find. 'And then we have to find out one new fact about the land or the creatures in it.'

The dragon on her left hand squeaked a few times.

'No, we haven't found anything out yet,' said Emily, understanding. 'We'll have to try and find something out tomorrow before we go back to school.'

The dragon said something to his friend. They flew off her hands and suddenly both started to sing in croaky voices! As they did so, a swirl of colours burst out of their mouths and formed two rainbows over their heads. Emily gasped. 'I didn't know ice dragons could do that!'

The dragons stopped singing and looked at her almost smugly.

Emily realized what she'd just said. 'You're showing me so that it can be our secret fact! Oh, wow! Thank you!'

The dragons chirruped happily at her.

She turned and ran back into the hut.
Wait until she told the others!

Hannah and Molly were delighted. 'I
wish I'd seen them do that,' said Molly.

'Me too,' said Hannah.

'We could ask them to show you
tomorrow,' said Emily, glancing out of
the window. 'It's dark now.'

'And the food is ready,' said Hannah.
'Let's eat. I'm starving.'

Molly had found some plates and they sat down on their beds and ate with the plates on their knees.

It was fun sitting in the warm hut with the dark night outside. Molly started telling scary stories. First of all, she made up stories about a creepy ice ghost who stalked his way through the woods at night and then she told them one about a boy who had found a ring beside a grave. She insisted on turning all the lights off apart from one as she told it.

'And, when the boy was in bed, he heard footsteps on the stairs and a voice saying, "I'm on the first step, Tommy, and I want my ring back." And then there was a thud on the next stair and the voice said, "I'm on the second step, Tommy,

and I want my ring back." And then there
was a thud on the last step and –'

There was a loud cracking noise as
something hit the window.

'Aaah!' Emily, Hannah and Molly all
jumped about a metre into the air.

'What was that?' gasped Hannah.

There was another noise and a ghostly
white shape flitted past the glass.

'Look!' Emily cried.

'It's a ghost!' yelled Hannah.

There was another crack as something
hit the window again. Emily and Hannah
both shrieked.

But Molly jumped to her feet and
went over to the side of the window. She
peered out. 'It's not a ghost. It's just
someone in a sheet trying to scare us!'

Emily felt her heart slow down. 'Really?'

'Yes. I can see a couple of other people in the shadows. The noise is them throwing pebbles at the window, I'm sure.'

Hannah got to her feet and joined Molly. 'You're right.' She looked cross. 'How dumb of them. They shouldn't be out in the dark.'

She marched to the door and opened it, with Molly and Emily behind her. 'Ha ha, very funny!' she called.

'Like we're scared,' added Molly.

'You so were!' came Camilla's smug voice out of the dark. She stepped forward out of the shadows of the trees. 'We heard you scream. You thought Tess really was a ghost.'

Tess had pulled off the sheet and was smirking at them. 'Tricked you!'

Molly snorted. 'No, you didn't. We

only screamed cos for a moment we thought it was . . . the ice ghost.'

'Ice ghost?' echoed Helena, who was beside Camilla with Clare. Emily could see the dragons stirring in the trees behind them, disturbed by all the noise. They peered over the twigs curiously, looking from one set of girls to the other.

'Yeah. Hadn't you heard about him? Madame Li told me. He's really tall and made of slabs of ice. He comes through the trees at night and grabs people,' said Molly. 'That was why Madame Letsworth said we had to stay in our shelters at night-time.'

'As if we're going to believe *that*,' said Camilla scornfully.

But the others looked a bit uncertain. 'Come on, Cam. Let's get back,' said Tess.

'You know what he does,' said Molly
quickly. 'He makes a singing sound and
makes rainbows appear in the air just before
he's about to grab someone, doesn't he,
Emily?' She gave Emily a meaningful look.

Emily stared at her and suddenly
realized what Molly wanted her to do.
'Oh, yes, that's what he does,' she said,
nodding hard. She looked at the dragons

and then whistled and chirruped, hoping she was getting the words right: '*Would you sing for me? Please!*'

Camilla stared at her. 'What's with all the whistling? You are so weird, Emily.'

'I might be weird, but at least I'm not out in the woods with the ice ghost,' said Emily as, to her delight, the dragons nodded. They lifted their snouts and began to sing.

Camilla instantly jumped at the croaking noise. 'What's that?'

'Camilla! Look!' cried Tess as rainbows of colour arched into the dark night sky above the dragons' nests.

Helena and Clare screamed.

'It's the ice ghost!' shouted Tess. 'It's come to get us!'

'Quick!' yelled Helena.

She, Clare and Tess raced through the trees. Camilla hesitated for a moment and then turned and ran after them as fast as she could.

Emily, Hannah and Molly fell about laughing. 'Oh, thank you!' Molly said to the dragons when they stopped singing.

'Yes, that was brilliant,' Emily said. 'Thank you so much!'

'Did you see Camilla's face?' chuckled Hannah.

The dragons looked amused. They chirruped a goodnight and settled down in their nests again.

Emily, Hannah and Molly went back inside their shelter still giggling. They cleared away their plates, got into their pyjamas and brushed their teeth. Then they snuggled down in their sleeping bags. 'We must get up early,' said Hannah. 'Just one more thing to get and then we can go back to school.'

'Oh, I hope we win!' said Emily.

'Sleep well,' said Molly. 'Don't let the ice ghosts bite!'

Giggling, they snuggled down and were soon fast asleep.

Chapter Eight
Race to School!

Emily, Hannah and Molly were up early the next morning. They got dressed and ate a quick breakfast of dried fruit and chocolate and then packed their bags. 'Just the leaf to get and then we go back to school as fast as we can,' said Molly.

Hannah showed them where they had to go on the map. 'Now, the most sensible way would be to ski across to the

big river over there and then skate down
that and along the main east river until
we get to where the burning bushes are,'
she said, pointing out a long route on the
winding big river. She glanced at Molly,
who looked as if she was about to say
something but then just nodded. Hannah
grinned. 'But we do want to win after all!
So why don't we try and take a short cut?'

'A short cut?' echoed Molly and Emily.

'Yeah, if we ski south and then join the little river that we skated here on, we can skate down it to the east. Then there's another small river off it that seems to lead straight to where the burning bushes are. It's a risk, but let's do it!'

'Cool!' said Molly in delight.

They shut the hut up and put their skis on. There had been more snow in the night and it lay on the ground thick and soft. Emily skied over to the dragons. 'Bye!' she called softly. 'Thank you for last night!'

One of the dragons poked his head up through the layer of snow on the nest. He chirruped.

'Yep, I'll tell the dragons at school about you,' promised Emily and then she joined the others.

They swished over the fresh snow, passing Camilla's hut. It was all shut up.

'They must have left already,' fretted Molly.

'I hope we beat them back,' said Emily. Now they were so near to the end of the scavenger hunt, she really wanted to win.

They reached the river they had skated down the day before and changed from their skis into their skates. As they did so, they heard voices.

Tasha and Olivia came skating round the bend going in the opposite direction to them. 'It shouldn't take us long to get there,' Tasha was saying.

'I hope it's not too hard to get a reed from the pools,' said Olivia. They caught sight of Emily, Hannah and Molly and waved.

Emily wondered where Amanda was, but just then Amanda came skating round the bend after them. 'Wait!' she was calling. 'My legs are tired. Stop going so fast, you two.'

Emily saw Olivia and Tasha exchange fed-up looks and they sped up. Amanda tried to go faster, but caught her skate on a bump in the ice and stumbled. She could have stayed on her feet – she was a really good skater – but she just seemed to give up and fall over. 'Wait!' she called plaintively from the ice. But the others had skated on round the next bend.

'I'm glad she's not in our team,' Molly muttered.

'I know she moans, but she's not that bad,' Emily said. She saw that Amanda

was looking really upset. 'Are you OK?'
she called.

Amanda didn't answer.

Emily left her things on the bank of
the river and skated over. 'Amanda?' She
offered her hand to help her up.

'Thanks,' Amanda muttered, getting to
her feet. 'They're mean. I'm never going
to catch up with them,' she said, wiping
the back of her hand across her eyes. 'They

keep skating off whenever I get near.'

Emily could understand why the others might be doing that. Amanda could be so annoying, but it still wasn't very nice of them. 'You skate fast. You'll catch up,' she said.

Amanda shook her head. 'I don't want to. I'm just going to go back to school.'

Emily frowned. 'You can't. Not on your own.'

'I'm not going after them,' said Amanda.

'Come on, Em. We should go!' Hannah called.

'Look, we're heading back towards school now,' said Emily quickly to Amanda. 'At least come with us. We've just got to get the leaf from the burning bush. That's all.' She remembered what had happened to Molly the day before when she'd gone off. 'You mustn't go off on your own – please.'

Amanda gave Emily a small smile. 'OK. Thanks.'

Emily could tell the others weren't that pleased with her for inviting Amanda to skate with them, but whether it was because they were heading back towards school or because Amanda was feeling grateful, she didn't moan at all and she even proved useful. 'No, don't go down that river,' she said when they reached the river that Hannah had been planning to take. 'It's blocked by a fallen tree. We tried to skate down it yesterday and had to come back in the end. I'll show you the way we went.'

'Thanks, Amanda,' said Hannah.

Amanda led the way and then turned

down a different small river. 'This one was clear yesterday.'

They all raced down it.

After about ten minutes they saw a glow of golden light ahead of them. 'Are those the burning bushes?' Molly asked Amanda.

Amanda nodded. 'They're amazing!'

As they got closer, they saw bushes dotted through the trees that looked like

they were being consumed by golden flames.

'How do we get a leaf?' said Hannah.

'We wondered that yesterday, but the flames aren't hot,' said Amanda. 'They're icy cold. So long as you've got gloves on, you can just pick a leaf.'

'I'll do it!' said Molly. She skated to the edge of the bank and found the nearest bush. 'Here goes!' She stuck her hand in. 'Got one!' she cried, holding out a leaf that looked like it was made from beaten gold.

'That's all the things on the list!' said Hannah. 'Now, we just need to get back.'

Emily's eyes shone. 'Come on! Let's go!'

Chapter Nine
And the Winner Is . . .

Emily, Hannah and Molly raced off down
the river with Amanda following behind.
They had seen from the map that it soon
joined up with the main river to the east
of the school. Once they were on that
river, all they would have to do was skate
for five minutes and they would be back.

But will we be first? Emily wondered.

Reaching the junction with the main

east river, they spotted another team heading towards them. It was Camilla, Tess, Clare and Helena! From the determined looks on their faces it looked as if they had found everything and were racing back to the school too.

Camilla caught sight of Emily and the others. 'Faster!' she yelled to her team.

'Quick!' gasped Molly.

Emily, Hannah and Molly turned on to

the river and started to skate as fast as
they could.

'Good luck!' called Amanda, not even
trying to keep up.

Emily crouched low. She had Hannah
on one side and Molly on the other.
They were in the lead, but behind them
she could hear the swish of skates.
Camilla and the others got closer and
closer, yelling encouragements to each
other as the river widened out.

'Faster!' gasped Hannah. 'We can't let
them win!'

Emily pushed her tired legs harder. Her
rucksack was digging into her shoulders,
but she ignored it. Now she could see the
lake behind the school just ahead of them
and the teachers waiting on it. The first
team on to the lake would be the winner.

Were they going to make it? No, Camilla and Tess were drawing alongside them.

Molly put on a burst of speed. Then Camilla caught up with her and drew ahead. Molly went faster. Camilla caught her again. They both put their heads down and skated as fast as they could. At the exact same moment they both zoomed on to the lake with everyone else only centimetres behind.

It had been a dead heat between the two teams!

Emily straightened up, letting her breath out in a rush of relief. She glided on both feet until she slowed down almost to a stop, then she skated round in a circle and met up with Hannah and Molly.

'Oh, wow, wasn't that amazing?' said Hannah, her eyes sparkling after the race.

'Brilliant!' said Molly. 'I wonder who'll be the winner.'

'I guess it depends if Camilla's team have got all their things,' said Emily.

'I don't actually care about winning now, you know,' said Hannah. 'It's been the most amazing couple of days. I've never had so much fun!'

Emily grinned at her. 'More fun than staying here and practising your double jumps?'

Hannah grinned back. 'Much more! I was so dumb. I can't believe I didn't want to do this.'

Madame Letsworth skated towards them all. 'Well done, girls. You are the first two teams back. Bring your things over and we'll see if we have a winning team or if it's a draw.'

Both teams skated to the group of teachers and got out the objects they had collected. As they did so, Tilda's team also arrived back and gathered round.

Emily watched eagerly as Madame Letsworth and Madame Li checked the things they had found – the icicle, the reed, the feather and the leaf. All the other teachers looked on with interest and some of the frost fairies flew around their heads.

'Congratulations,' said Madame Letsworth, smiling round at both Emily and Camilla's teams. 'If both teams have found out something true then it will be a draw.'

Camilla tossed her hair. 'Well, our fact's true.'

'So, what did you find out?' Madame Longley asked her.

'We found out about ice ghosts!' burst out Tess.

'Yes, they make a rainbow appear in the air just before they arrive and grab you,' said Camilla smugly. She glanced at Emily's team as if to say *Beat that!*

Emily bit her lip to stop herself smiling.

Madame Letsworth's eyebrows rose.

'*What* did you say you found out, Camilla?'

Camilla repeated it slightly less certainly. 'That ice ghosts make a strange noise and a rainbow of light appears before they try and grab you and scare you?'

A snort of laughter burst from Molly. Emily and Hannah giggled too.

Camilla turned on her crossly. 'What? You were there too. You saw it.'

Madame Letsworth looked like she was trying to hide a smile. 'I don't think so, Camilla. There are no such things as ice ghosts, you see.'

Camilla frowned. 'But . . . but . . .'

Molly giggled. 'Shall we tell you our fact, Madame?'

Madame Letsworth nodded.

'Emily?' said Molly.

'It's that ice *dragons* can make rainbows

appear over their heads when they sing,'
said Emily.

'Well, that is certainly true,' said
Madame Letsworth, her eyes twinkling as
she looked at Camilla.

Camilla's eyes widened. 'That noise . . .
those rainbows . . . they were from *ice
dragons*?'

Molly, Hannah and Emily nodded.
'Yep!' said Molly.

'No!' Camilla stamped her foot in rage.

Madame Letsworth cleared her throat.
'Well, seeing as Emily, Hannah and Molly
came back with a true fact, I declare their
team to be the winning team and the
three of them to be the winners of the
scarlet skates. We were watching all the
teams through crystal balls similar to the
ones we gave you and I have to say we

were very impressed with the way you worked together, girls, and with your kindness, Emily. You helped someone out even though she wasn't on your team and, throughout the two days, you have shown that you are very much in tune with the land. Well done!'

Emily glowed with delight.

Madame Letsworth clapped her hands. 'To the winners of the scarlet skates!' Everyone apart from Camilla's team clapped. 'We'll present them to you later this morning,' Madame Letsworth said.

Emily, Hannah and Molly hugged each other. Emily caught sight of Amanda watching.

'Thank you,' Emily said, breaking away and skating over to her. 'We wouldn't have got back in time to win if you hadn't told us about the river.'

'Thanks for letting me skate back with you,' said Amanda gratefully. 'I really didn't want to come back on my own.'

There was the sound of voices and Tasha and Olivia came skating on to the lake. They were very relieved to see Amanda. 'We were wondering where you were!' Tasha gasped. 'We've been looking for you everywhere. We didn't get the feather in the end. We used the crystal ball to tell Madame Li you were lost and she said you were OK and back here.'

'I'm sorry we left you,' Olivia said, looking guilty.

'We have our runners-up,' Madame Longley announced. 'Tilda, Alice, Zoe and Heather have all the objects and another true fact. They found out that snow foxes can sleep in trees.'

Camilla's team looked furious. They hadn't even been runners-up!

'And now I'm sure you're all ready for some hot chocolate and cake,' said Madame Letsworth. 'It'll be served in ten minutes in the common room.'

Camilla's team skated off grumpily and the teachers went inside. Hannah, Molly and Emily shrugged off their rucksacks. It was a relief not to have the weight on their shoulders any more. Enjoying the lightness, Emily skated away in a big circle and Hannah and Molly sped after her.

'We won!' Molly said in delight.

'We got the scarlet skates!' said Emily.

'And we had so much fun,' said Hannah.

'Though we didn't find out any more about the Ice Princess or if there is a dragon in the mountains,' Molly pointed out.

'Next week, we will,' Hannah declared. She skated forward and threw herself into a double toe loop followed smoothly by a double flip. Relaxed and happy, she landed both jumps perfectly.

Emily and Molly cheered.

'Let's play follow-my-leader,' shouted Molly.

They got in a line. Emily saw Amanda watching, almost enviously, as they skated after Molly trying to do an Egyptian dance. 'Come on, Amanda, join in!'

Amanda hesitated.

'Yeah, come on, Amanda,' called Molly. 'We wouldn't have won the competition if it wasn't for you. Join in with us!'

Hannah nodded too, and Amanda smiled and skated over. They took it in turns to be the leader and go round on the lake until they were dizzy with laughter.

Then they split up and all started jumping and spinning round on the ice. Hannah skated faster and faster and threw herself into a double lutz jump. Molly turned into the fastest layback spin that Emily had ever seen and Amanda jumped a single axel.

Emily felt joy rush through her. They had won the competition and the scarlet skates and they'd had so much fun. They might not have found out much more about the Ice Princess, but they would. She knew they would.

Bubbling with happiness, she put her arms above her head and began to spin. *There's nothing better than being here at ice-skating school*, she thought as the world blurred to a sparkling white around her. *Nothing at all!*

Do you dream of becoming an Ice Princess?

Have you ever wanted to go to a REAL Skating School?

All readers of *Skating School* get FREE membership to the National Ice Skating Association's Skate UK programme!

Skate UK will help you to learn all the moves and basic skills you need to become a true Ice Princess! It's all about fun and continuous movement and is taught in groups, so why not share your love of *Skating School* with your friends and bring them too?

To get your free membership, go to
www.iceskating.org.uk/skatingschool
and enter the secret password: **Twirl**.

Skate UK is taught by licensed NISA coaches and can be assisted by trained Programme Assistants.

For full terms and conditions visit:
www.lindachapman.co.uk
www.iceskating.org.uk/skatingschool

Do you want to enter super competitions, get sneak previews and download lots of *Skating School* fun?

Get YOUR skates on
join the
Sparkle Club
today!
lindachapman.co.uk

Just enter this secret password:

Twirl

The Land of Ice and Winter is waiting for you ...

Design your own ice-skating dress!

The tiny frost fairies have been working overtime designing the beautiful dresses for the girls to wear in the Ice-skating Academy competitions.

Using this dress as a template, the fairies need you to draw the most magical ice-skating outfit you can think of. Every month one lucky winner will receive a magical *Skating School* goody bag!

Send your drawing

with your name and address to:

Skating School Competition, Puffin Marketing, 80 Strand, London WC2R 0RL

Or e-mail them to: **skatingschool@uk.penguingroup.com**

Welcome back to the magical Land of Ice and Winter

... a world where all your dreams come true!

A magical world of whirling on ice!

Skating School

Linda Chapman

A brand-new

Skating School series

Coming soon!

Hi there,

I hope you've enjoyed reading about the adventures of the girls who go to the Magic Ice-skating Academy. I love writing them all down! Wouldn't it be amazing to go to the Land of Ice and Winter and see all the creatures who live there? Can you imagine holding an actual ice dragon or talking to a frost fairy?

Sometimes readers write to me and ask about my life. Being a writer is the best job ever. I live in a cottage in a village with my family and two dogs – a Bernese mountain dog and a golden retriever. I spend my days writing and going to visit schools and libraries to talk about writing.

I always think I'm really lucky because I get to spend my days writing about magic – mermaids, unicorns, stardust spirits, genies and now the Land of Ice and Winter. If you love them too then why not go to **www.lindachapman.co.uk** and join the Sparkle Club? It's my online fan club with loads of activities and downloads, and you can only get to it by using the secret password at the back of this book. Have fun!

Love,

Linda
xxx